SHOE DOG

story by Megan McDonald • pictures by Katherine Tillotson

A Richard Jackson Book

Atheneum Books for Young Readers   New York London Toronto Sydney New Delhi

For Katherine,
whose original painting
of Shoe Dog
inspired this story
—M. M.

For Megan
—K. T.

A
atheneum

ATHENEUM BOOKS FOR YOUNG READERS
An imprint of Simon & Schuster Children's Publishing Division
1230 Avenue of the Americas, New York, New York 10020
Text copyright © 2014 by Megan McDonald
Illustrations copyright © 2014 by Katherine Tillotson
ATHENEUM BOOKS FOR YOUNG READERS is a registered trademark of
Simon & Schuster, Inc.
Atheneum logo is a trademark of Simon & Schuster, Inc.
For information about special discounts for bulk purchases, please
contact Simon & Schuster Special Sales at 1-866-506-1949 or
business@simonandschuster.com.
The Simon & Schuster Speakers Bureau can bring authors to your
live event. For more information or to book an event, contact the
Simon & Schuster Speakers Bureau at 1-866-248-3049 or visit our
website at www.simonspeakers.com.
Book design by Ann Bobco and Katherine Tillotson
The text for this book is set in Hank BT.
The illustrations for this book were created with
crayon and charcoal and combined digitally.
Manufactured in China
0614 SCP
2 3 4 5 6 7 8 9 10
Library of Congress Cataloging-in-Publication Data
McDonald, Megan.
Shoe dog / Megan McDonald ; pictures by Katherine Tillotson. —
1st. ed.
p. cm
"A Richard Jackson Book."
Summary: In order to stay in the warm and cozy home he has
longed for, Shoe Dog must learn to stop chewing shoes.
ISBN 978-1-4169-7932-6 (hardcover)
ISBN 978-1-4169-8588-4 (eBook)
[1. Dog adoption—Fiction. 2. Dogs—Training—Fiction.]
I. Tillotson, Katherine, illustrator. II. Title.
PZ7.M478419Sho 2014
[E]—dc23
2012051499

Ooh, look at the puppy!
Who's a good boy?
You're so cute. Yes, you are!

He perked up an ear at the kitchee-coo words.

Dog wanted a home.
A real home.
A place full of
hundreds of nose kisses,
dozens of tummy rubs.
A place as warm as soup
and cozy as pie.

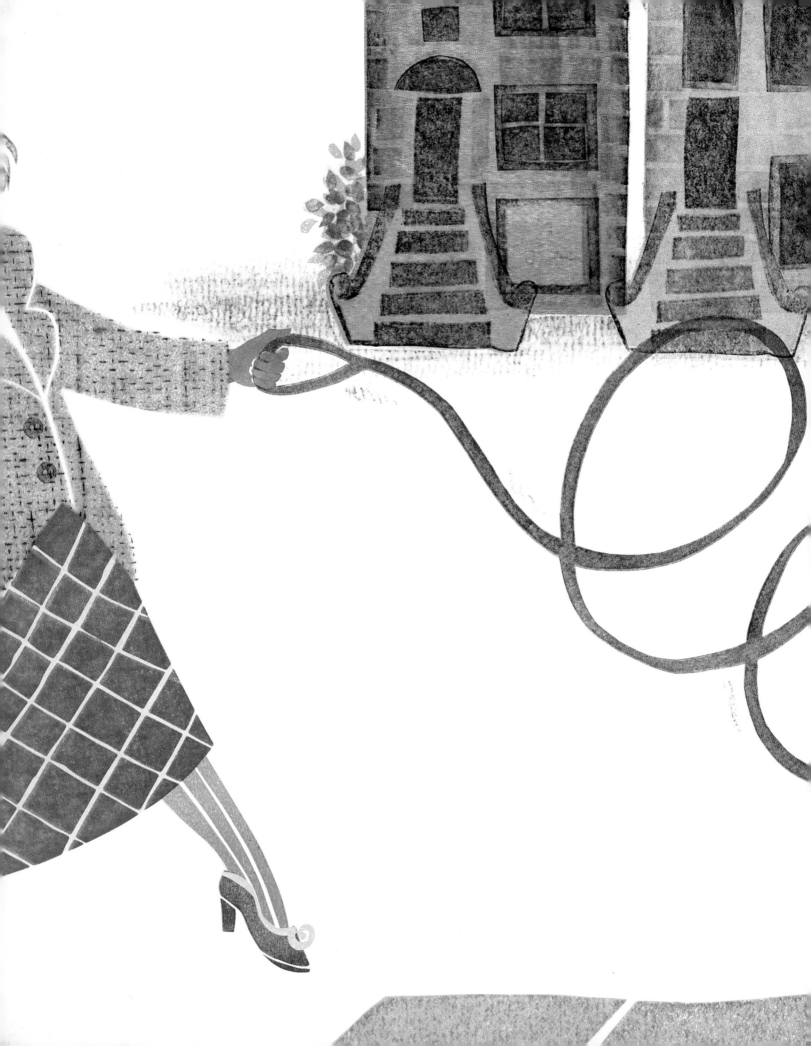

A place with room to run . . .

. . . and things to chew.

But he did not want
a boring old bone,
a squeaky old toy,
a smelly old sock.

No!

He wanted . . .

. . . a shoe!

Shoe Dog!

She, Herself called him.

You're so cute, but . . .

That very day,
Shoe Dog chewed through
five high heels,
four flip-flops,
three sneakers,
two boots,
one wing tip.

BAD DOG!

She, Herself said.

That night,
Shoe Dog slept
at the bottom
of the Big Bed.
She did not give Shoe Dog
one ear scratch or head pat.
Not one tummy rub.
Not a single nose kiss.

The next day,
She came home with
a New Box.
Not a big box.
Not a little box.
A just-right box
with Noisy Paper inside.

Grr!

Shoe Dog nosed open the lid.
He rustled and tussled
with the Noisy Paper. . . .

New Shoes!

BAD DOG!

She, Herself wagged and pointed.

Shoe Dog had to spend a long while
on the Corner Rug
with not one thing to chew.

That night,
Shoe Dog did not sleep
on the Big Bed
with the Cozy Covers
in the Land of Upstairs.
But . . .

. . . the very next day
She came home with
another New Box.

Not a big box.
Not a little box.
A just-right box.
This time
She took it straight
to the Land of Upstairs.

Shoe Dog turned circles.
Shoe Dog jumped at the gate.
Shoe Dog jumped
over the gate!

He raced up the stairs,
ba-doom, ba-doom.

Sniff! Sniff!
He sniffed here,

here,

and everywhere.

There!
On the bed
was the New Box
and inside
the box was . . .

. . . a
brand
new
pair
of
shoes!

Shoe Dog settled down
between the arms
of Comfy Chair
in the Land of Upstairs
to have himself
a good chew.

BAD BAD DOG!

She, Herself said.

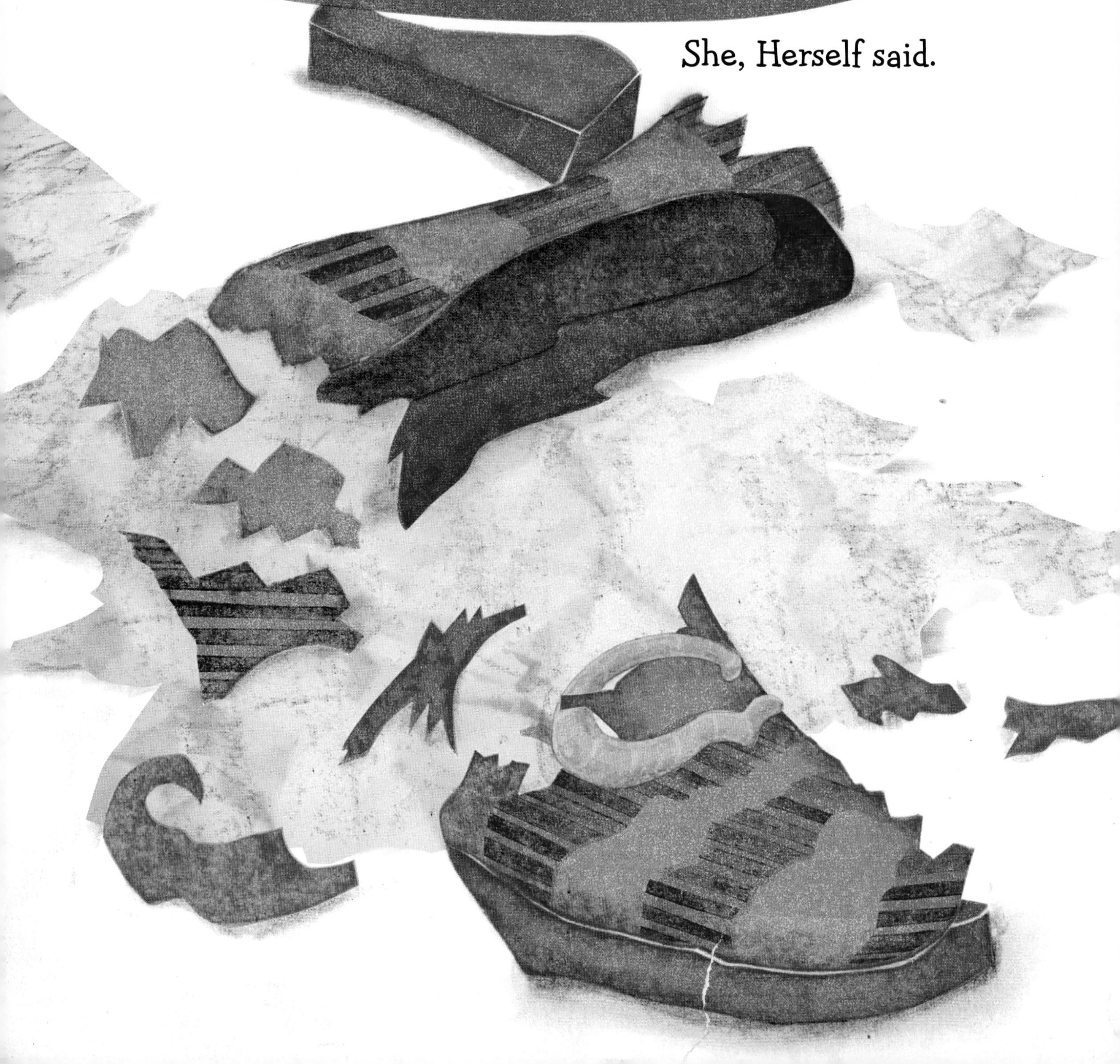

That night,
Shoe Dog slept
downstairs
on the cold, cold floor
with only a mop
for a friend.

Shoe Dog did not want to go back
to the Land of Sad Puppies
and Scratched-Up Cats
and One-Eared Bunnies.
No!

For the next long while,
Shoe Dog was a Good Dog.
He did not chew so much
as a fleabite.

Then one day,
She, Herself came home
with a great big
munchy-crunchy,
crinkly-wrinkly,
Bright Shiny Bag
full of one-two-three
New Boxes.
She took the Big Bag
up the stairs.
Shoe Dog lifted an eyebrow,
twitched a whisker,
perked up an ear.

Was it?
Could it be?
Shoe Dog was sure
he heard
the friendly rustle-bustle
of Noisy Paper. . . .

Shoe Dog raced up
the stairs again,
ba-doom, ba-doom.

Sniff! Sniff! Sniff!
He sniffed beneath the Big Bed.
No shoes.

He sniffed all around
Comfy Chair.
No shoes.

He sniffed under the Forest of Dresses.
No shoes.

There!
Way up high
on a tippy-top shelf
above the Forest of Dresses
was the Bright Shiny Bag
with box
after

box
after
box
inside.

Shoe Dog leaped onto
Comfy Chair.

He pulled
and pawed
and tugged
and lugged
and . . .

CRASH!

Down came Bright Shiny Bag.

Down came a tumble of boxes.

Down came a jumble of Noisy Paper,

shoes and all!

Shoe Dog stood still.
Shoe Dog stared.
Shoe Dog sniffed.

No!
Shoe Dog
did not
would not
could not
ever
chew
this
new
shoe!

She, Herself heard the crash
and came running.
She stood still.
She stared.

Shoe Dog rubbed noses with Shoe Cat.
Shoe Dog tickled whiskers with Shoe Cat.

Shoe Dog gave Shoe Cat a lick, lick, lick,
then a slurp,
then a great
big
doggie
slobber kiss.

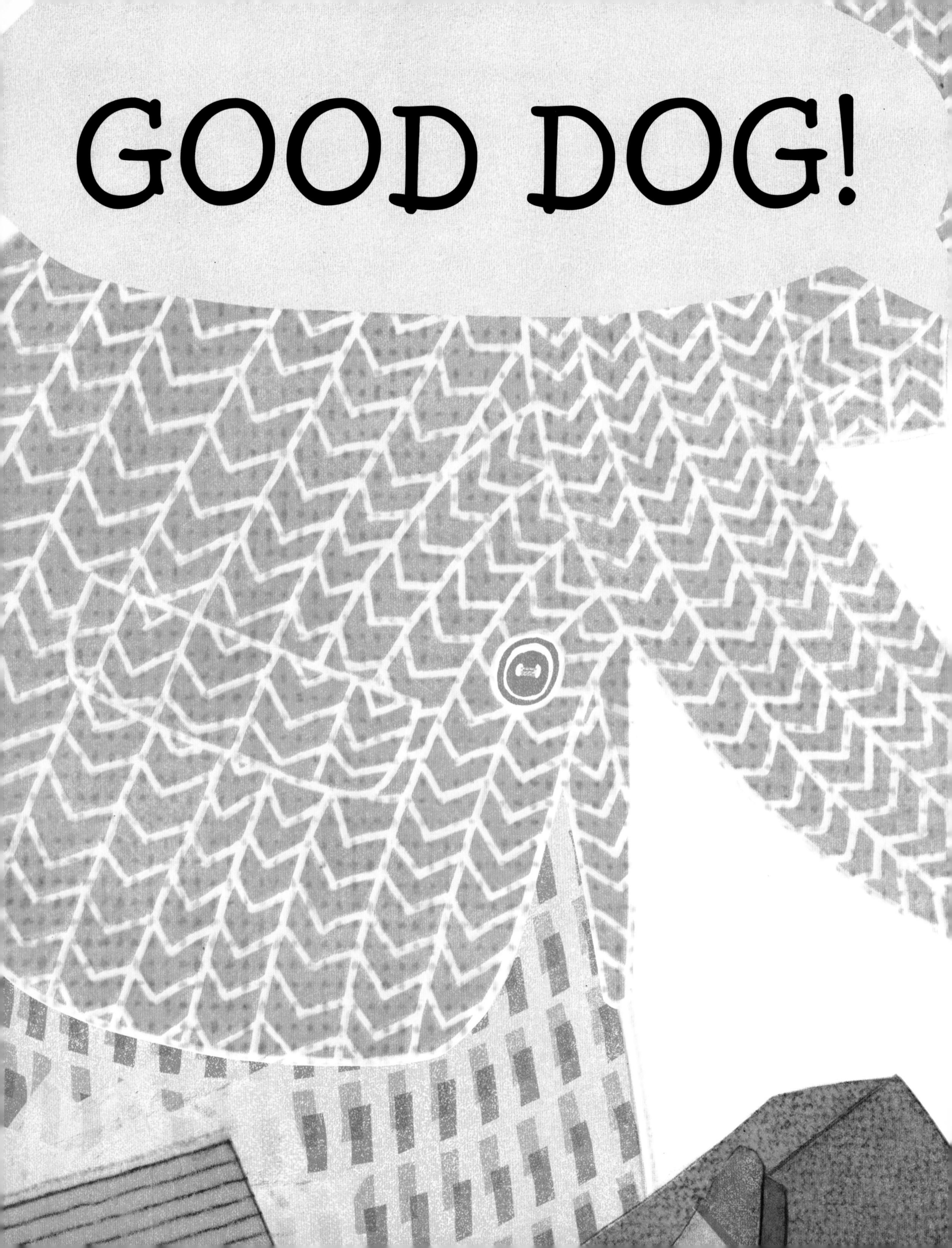
GOOD DOG!

She scratched his ears
and patted his head.
She rubbed his tummy,
and kissed Shoe Dog
right
on
the
nose.

That night, Shoe Dog jumped
on the Big Bed
in the Land of Upstairs . . .

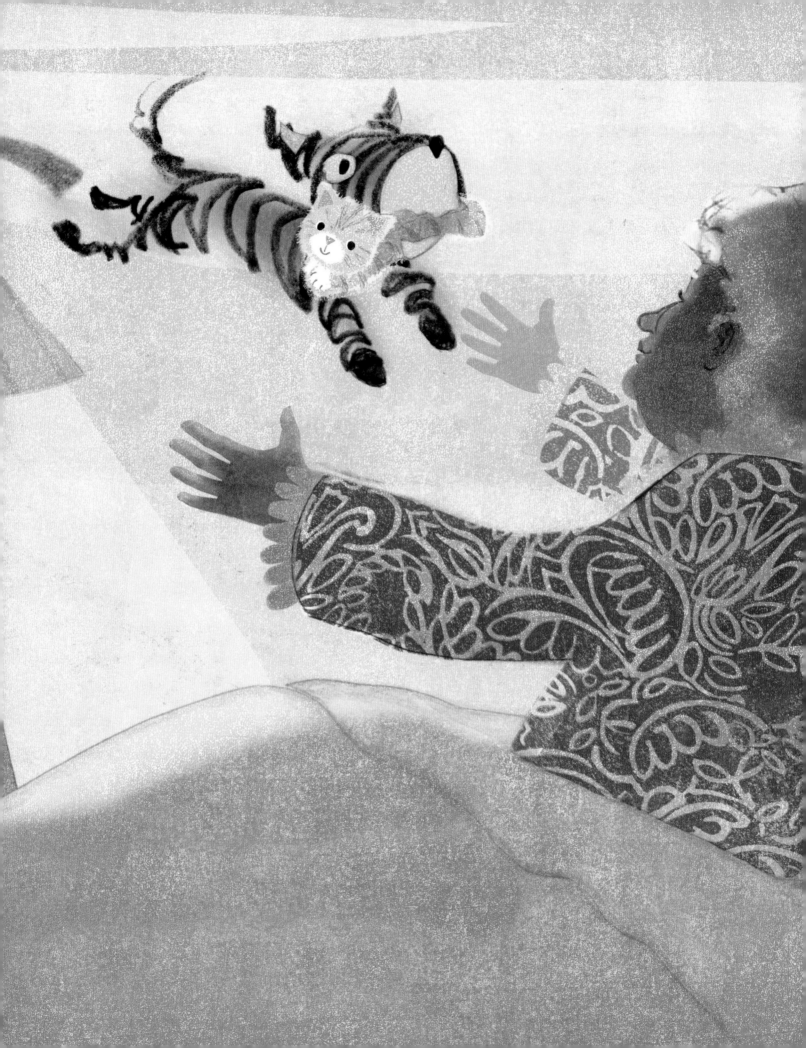

. . . and curled up
with his
new
found
friend
until the two were
warm as soup,
cozy as pie.